# Woodland Magic

## THE STRANDED OTTER

# JULIE SYKES

*illustrated by* KATY RIDDELL

Piccadilly
PRESS

First published in Great Britain in 2023 by
PICCADILLY PRESS
4th Floor, Victoria House, Bloomsbury Square, London WC1B 4DA
Owned by Bonnier Books
Sveavägen 56, Stockholm, Sweden
www.piccadillypress.co.uk

Text copyright © Julie Sykes, 2023
Illustrations copyright © Katy Riddell, 2023

A CIP catalogue record for this book is available from the British Library.

ISBN: 978-1-80078-144-3
*Also available as an ebook and in audio*

1

Typeset by Envy Design Ltd
Printed and bound in Great Britain by Clays Ltd, Elcograf S.p.A.

Piccadilly Press is an imprint of Bonnier Books UK
www.bonnierbooks.co.uk

# Woodland Magic

## THE STRANDED OTTER

# THE WOODLAND MAGIC SERIES

# Chapter One

'Is it ready?' asked Cora.

A wooden raft lay on the bank of the stream that ran through the Hidden Middle of the Whispering Woods.

'Not quite.' Trix walked around the raft, occasionally stopping to tweak a vine or tighten a wooden screw.

'What's taking so long?' Jax asked.

'It has to be safe.'

Cora glanced at the other rafts already floating in the stream. None of them were as good as theirs. 'It won't sink, Trix. You're a genius,' she said proudly.

Cora and her friends Jax, Trix and Nis had finished their early morning rewilding tasks in the Big Outside and were working on their raft. Every year Grandmother Sky, the Queen of the Hidden Middle, celebrated her birthday with a raft race followed by a party by moonlight. It was the first time that Cora and her friends had been old enough to race and they couldn't wait. Trix, who loved making things, had designed the raft by herself.

Trix turned pink. She pushed her screwdriver into her bun for safekeeping and wiped her hands down her woven grass jeans. 'Let's get it in the water.'

The raft was made from a lattice of hollow reeds topped with a wooden platform. It had four bark seats, two at the front and two at the back. A leaf canopy, supported by twigs, gave the crew shelter from the sun or rain. Four wooden paddles were strapped to the deck with a vine.

Cora, Jax, Trix and Nis each stood at a corner, ready to lift it up.

'Hi, lo, GO!' said Trix.

'Fizzing frogs, it's heavy!' Cora grunted. Her arms ached as she shuffled towards the water, carrying her corner of the raft.

'Jax, too fast,' Trix warned. 'We're not racing yet!'

'Sorry!' Jax slowed down.

When they reached the stream, Trix shouted instructions as they carefully

lowered the raft into the water. A plaited vine rope allowed the raft to be tied to something on the bank, to stop it from floating away. Trix passed the rope to Cora. 'Hold this.'

The raft dipped as Trix stepped aboard. She untied the paddles and put one by each seat.

Cora held her breath and the rope. 'It floats!' she exclaimed when Trix was safely aboard.

A beaming Trix took her place at the back. Nis went aboard next, followed by Jax. At last, it was Cora's turn. She put a foot on the raft then stopped.

'Cattywumps! That poor caddisfly.'

A grey moth-like insect with hairy wings was floating on its back in the stream. Its legs waved feebly as it tried to right itself. Cora, one foot on shore, one on the raft, tucked

the rope under her arm as she reached to
rescue the caddisfly from the water. The
raft drifted away from the bank. The gap
between Cora's feet widened.

'Jump!' shouted Jax.

'Can't!' Cora's legs were doing the
splits as the raft floated further away from
the shore.

Jax knelt and held out his paddle to Cora.
'Hold the end and I'll pull you aboard.'

'What with?' Cora's hands were already
full of caddisfly. The distance between the
raft and the bank grew wider. Cora's legs
were stretched as far as they could go. She
cupped her fingers around the caddisfly and
leapt for the bank. Her foot slipped as she
jumped. Cora wobbled then fell. *Splash!* She
landed in the water, dropping the vine but
not the caddisfly. By holding her arm up she
managed to keep the half-drowned insect

out of the water. The stream was shallow enough for Cora to stand up in. Finding her feet, she waded to the bank, where she put the caddisfly on the grass to dry.

Was it still alive? A wing twitched. Cora's heart fluttered.

'Don't give up, little one. I can heal you with some woodland magic.' Cora pointed her fingers at the caddisfly and imagined the insect growing strong again. She wiggled her fingers, showering its wings with a sparkly magical mist. A pip later, the caddisfly struggled up. Its wings quivered. Then it flew, circling Cora, hovering in front of her nose as if to thank her, before flying away.

Cora sighed happily. She loved all animals, even the tiny ones.

'Well done, Cora.' From the raft, Jax, Nis and Trix tapped their thumbs together, congratulating her.

'Loser,' drawled a bored voice.

Cora looked up in surprise. Perfect Penelope floated past, lounging on a raft made from tree bark while her friend Winnie paddled furiously with a wooden oar.

'Eeew! Cora, you've got river weed tangled in your hair. Oh no, silly me! That *is* your hair.' Penelope cackled with laughter.

Cora ignored her. She didn't care if her long green hair was wet and tangled. She'd saved the caddisfly. That's what mattered.

Penelope didn't think so. 'I can't believe you wasted woodland magic on an ugly caddisfly.' She shuddered.

'A waste, is it?'

Cora looked up to see Scarlet Busybee striding towards the stream, her face like a thundercloud. 'All bugs are important, no matter what they look like. Nature Keepers care for *every living thing* no matter how small or unusual. Do I make myself clear?' Scarlet's eyes bored into Penelope's.

Penelope stared at her feet. 'Yes,' she muttered.

'Hmmm.' Scarlet didn't sound convinced. 'Where is your paddle? Help Winnie bring that raft back to the bank immediately. It's not safe. It needs to be more stable before you can take part in the race.'

Scarlet then turned her attention to Cora. Tapping her thumbs together she said, 'Good work, Cora.'

Cora's face warmed with the unexpected praise.

She and Jax had been working extra hard at their daily rewilding tasks in the Big Outside. A while ago, when Cora and Jax had built a hedgehog highway to allow hedgehogs to travel through a new housing estate, Scarlet had said they only needed to complete one more rewilding task successfully and then she would make them both fully trained Nature Keepers.

However, Cora and Jax had completed many successful missions since then, but Scarlet still hadn't promoted them. Cora was beginning to think that Scarlet, who never forgot anything, was going to send them back to school. But why? She wanted to ask Scarlet, only each time she tried, her heart fluttered like the caddisfly's wings and she couldn't get her words out.

'Cora.' Scarlet was still talking to her. 'Please be more careful in future. I don't

have time to rescue you if you drown.'
Turning away abruptly, Scarlet went to
join her assistant Haru, who was perched
on a log further upstream, whittling a piece
of wood.

Cora sighed deeply. It wasn't fair.
Penelope was only a fully trained Keeper
because Winnie had helped her. Winnie
often did Perfect Penelope's work for her.
But Cora wasn't a tell-tale nit. 'I'll just have
to work even harder,' she vowed.

# Chapter Two

At breakfast the following morning Cora ate quickly, sharing her bark-bread toast with Nutmeg, her friendly mouse, when Mum wasn't looking.

'I'm off now,' Cora said as she shrugged her shoulders into her woodland bag.

'Me too.' Mum rarely went rewilding in the Big Outside. Instead, she worked with Nis's dad in the Crow's Nest, the Keepers' favourite cafe. 'Stay safe, keep out of sight and don't get caught by the Ruffins.'

'Always!' Cora ran down the wooden staircase that spiralled round the outer trunk of their treetop home. Jax arrived as she reached the bottom.

'Ready?' he asked.

'Ready,' said Cora.

They raced each other to the Bramble Door. Jax won by a nose. Penelope and Winnie arrived behind them.

'Out of the way, trainees,' said Penelope loudly.

Cora pretended not to hear.

Scarlet was at the gate handing out rewilding tasks to the Keepers. She glanced up and her eyes narrowed. When Cora and Jax reached the front of the queue, Scarlet said, 'The results from our recent bug count are worryingly low. Bugs play an important part in the food chain. They also help to pollinate plants. Today's task, of building a bug hotel, is so important that I'm giving it to several Keepers. Cora and Jax, I want you to build a bug hotel by the new supermarket. The land there used to be rich in bugs, but the creatures were made homeless when it was cleared to build on. Penelope and Winnie, your task is the same and at the same place.'

Penelope's expression turned as sour as a sloe berry but Cora was delighted. They'd made bug hotels at school with Signor Dragonfly. It had been great fun. Here was an easy chance to show Scarlet they were good enough to become fully trained Keepers. Jax looked pleased too.

'On it!' Cora told Scarlet. She stepped towards the Bramble Gate.

Scarlet blocked her way. 'Wait for the Want and the Warning. Today's Want is food. Everything you can forage for

Grandmother Sky's moonlight party. The
tastier the better! *Stay out of sight and don't get
caught by the Ruffins.* Now you can go,'
she added.

With the Want and the Warning
delivered, Cora and Jax leapt through the
Bramble Door and into the Big Outside.
As they ran through the woods, Winnie's
voice floated after them. 'Wait.'

Cora pulled up sharply.
'What's up?'

Winnie caught
up with Cora
and Jax. Looking
suddenly shy,
she mumbled,
'I thought we
could build the
shelters together.

It'll be faster to work as a team and a lot more fun.'

Cora stared at Winnie in surprise. It was a good idea but . . .

'Not happening,' Penelope said crossly as she caught Winnie up. 'I will supervise the trainees but I'm not doing their work for them. Anyway, our bug hotel is going to be the biggest and the best.'

Cora and Jax exchanged a look.

'Tempting,' said Jax, his lips twitching as he tried not to laugh. 'The supervising.'

'As tempting as working with a Ruffin,' Cora said.

Cora and Jax doubled up laughing.

'Your loss!' Penelope stuck her nose in the air as she stalked away.

Winnie looked quite sad, but when Penelope called for her to hurry, she trotted after her.

'Not doing our work for us!' Cora raised her eyebrows at Jax. 'Penelope never does any work.'

'*Our bug hotel is going to be the biggest and the best,*' he mimicked. 'We'll show them. Our hotel is going to be huge.' He set off, running through the woods.

The Keepers rewilded to repair the countryside from all the damage done to it by the Ruffins. Rewilding wasn't a competition, but Jax loved to compete.

*Me too*, thought Cora. She was just as much up for the challenge.

It had rained overnight and the ground was soggy. Mud splattered Cora's jeans as she ran. She caught Jax up and they burst out of the woods and ran across the stone bridge arching over the river. When they reached the other side, they stopped to catch their breath.

'Look at it.' Cora had to shout to make herself heard above the crashing water as it hurtled past, carrying broken branches and leaves.

'Jax, careful!' she added, as he went to stand at the edge. The swollen river was the highest she'd ever seen it.

'What?' he said innocently. 'I won't fall in.'

'Like the time you didn't fall in when we were counting tadpoles?'

Jax chuckled. 'That wasn't my fault.'

'It never is,' Cora agreed with a smile. 'Trix and Nis helped me to get you out. If you fall in now, the water is too powerful for me to rescue you, even if the others were here to help.'

Jax stared longingly at the racing water. 'Wouldn't it be fun if we could have the raft race here?'

'In the Big Outside? What about the Ruffins?'

Jax shrugged. 'They're mostly tucked up in their houses at night. Think how fast the raft would go. Much quicker than sailing it on the stream in the Hidden Middle. We'd better go,' he said at last.

'Wait!' A flash of brown caught Cora's eye. She pointed with a long finger. 'What's that?'

A shadow moved beneath the surface of the water. As Cora tracked it, a sleek head surfaced.

'An otter!' Cora's eyes shone. She held her breath as the otter sliced through the choppy water with strong paws. Reaching the bank, it climbed out and disappeared into a den, the entrance almost concealed by trailing tree roots.

'Listen!' Cora cupped a hand to her pointy ear. 'Hear those squeaks? The otter has pups.' Cora's heart melted to a puddle. Otter pups were the cutest! If they waited a pip, they might come out to play.

'They sound hungry,' said Jax. 'Same here. Breakfast feels like a forest ago. Let's go build a bigger and better bug hotel than Penelope and Winnie. Then we can go to the Crow's Nest for something to eat.'

Reluctantly, Cora tore herself away. Jax was right. They should do their task before the sun rose and the Ruffins came out. They wouldn't become fully trained Keepers if they wasted time watching otters.

# Chapter Three

Cora and Jax ran on past the boathouse and the shuttered cafe. They crossed over the football pitch and stopped at the road. Cora's stomach wriggled like tadpoles. Ruffin roads were dangerous. A Ruffin riding in a car could flatten a Keeper even faster than a Ruffin stomping around on pongy feet.

'Check right, check left, repeat,' she whispered.

The road was clear.

'Yuck!' said Jax as he scampered across the empty tarmac. 'Nasty.'

Cora gritted her teeth. Jax wasn't the only one to hate the feel of the road under his feet. Earth was so much softer.

'Don't stop,' said Jax.

'Not stopping.' Cora clambered up the kerb. They ran along the pavement until they reached the new supermarket. Another road, this one curving, led round to a huge space with rectangular boxes painted on the ground in white.

'The boxes are where the Ruffins leave their cars,' said Jax knowingly.

The supermarket rose up before them. It was huge, with enormous glass windows. Nearby, another box painted on the ground was full of trolleys stacked together in long lines.

'Ruffin chariots,' said Cora.

Jax nodded. 'To carry the food to their cars. Remember that time we built wooden ones at school?'

Cora started to giggle. 'I remember chariot racing!'

'It wasn't my fault we crashed into Penelope.'

'Remember the paint and feathers? They were stuck in her hair for ages!' Cora doubled over with laughter.

'That bit might have been my fault,'
Jax admitted, cracking up.

When they'd recovered, Cora and Jax
stood on tiptoes with their noses pressed
against the window.

'Croaking crows!' gasped Jax. 'Look at
all that food.'

The supermarket was closed but Ruffins
had left the lights on inside. Near the door,
Cora could see a huge display of shiny fruit
and vegetables, some she'd never seen before.

'Is it real?' she asked. 'It all seems too
perfect. The stuff we find in the wild is
never that shiny.'

'They polish everything,' said Jax.

Cora shook her head. 'Weird!'

Jax shrugged. 'That's Ruffins for you.
Where shall we build our bug hotel?'

'Somewhere out of the way. We don't
want the Ruffins to stamp on it,' said Cora.

They walked around the building,
passing one small tree with flowers
growing around the base. They rounded
the corner and found another car park
behind the supermarket. The parking
spaces were much longer. There were no
windows in the back of the building, just
one huge metal door. There was also a
row of rectangular bins on wheels, with
piles of plastic crates stacked next to them.
Cora groaned. Winnie and Penelope were
standing by the crates, arguing.

'Food was on Scarlet's Want List,'
Winnie kept insisting.

'Food, not Ruffin leftovers,' said Penelope
scornfully. 'If it's not good enough for the
Ruffins to eat, then it's definitely not good
enough for me.' Penelope's face darkened
when she saw Cora and Jax. 'We're wasting
time,' she snapped. 'We should start on our

bug hotel. We're building it under the tree. The only tree here,' she added, throwing a triumphant look at Cora and Jax. 'You'll have to find somewhere else to put yours.'

Penelope patted her perfectly styled pink hair then marched back around the side of the building. Winnie hesitated. She looked as if she wanted to say something.

'Winnie, hurry,' called Penelope sharply.

Winnie sighed and hurried after her.

Jax grinned at Cora. 'Since Penelope has bagged the one and only tree, where do you want to build our hotel?'

Cora wasn't listening. She was busy examining the plastic crates. They were black with tiny square holes that Cora could see through. 'That's why Winnie and Penelope were arguing. Some of the crates contain food,' she said. 'Help me move them, Jax.'

Even the smallest crate tower was too tall and heavy for Cora and Jax to lift.

'We could use woodland magic,' said Cora.

They pointed their long fingers at a tower of crates.

'Hi, lo, GO!'

Together, they sprinkled the crates with magical mist, quickly jumping back as each crate at the top of the pile floated to the ground.

'Cattywumps! Look at this.' Cora leaned into a crate and lifted out a purple plum with both hands. 'It's not perfect or as shiny as the ones in the shop, but it still looks yummy. It's got a tiny bruise. I bet that's why the Ruffins didn't want it.'

'Their loss,' said Jax. He pulled a wonky carrot from another crate. 'I like the shape of this. It's got rabbit ears.'

Cora shrugged her woodland bag off her back and, opening it up, she carefully put the plum inside. 'What else is there?'

'I spy potato.' Jax popped the carrot and wonky looking potato into his bag.

Cora found an apple with a brown mark and a battered swede. Jax helped her to roll the swede into her bag.

'Woodland bags are the best,' said Cora.

Woodland bags were made from spiders' thread. They were silky soft, incredibly strong and infused with woodland magic, so they were stretchy and light to carry, no matter what you put inside them. A woodland bag could hold anything, even a Ruffin if you were brave enough to catch one!

'Scarlet's going to be thrilled with this haul,' said Jax, when all of the crates were empty. 'If we do a good job on the bug hotel, then she's got to pass us. We'll be fully trained Keepers at last!'

Cora crossed her finger over her thumb for good luck. 'Let's get started. Where shall we put our hotel?'

'There.' Jax pointed to a patch of brambles growing against a metal fence.

Cora nodded. 'Good choice. The brambles will hide it from the Ruffins and give the bugs extra places to live and find food.' As she spoke, an idea tumbled into her head. 'Jax! We should use a crate to make the hotel. Let's fill it with different materials to make different spaces for all kinds of bugs.'

'Why not use all of the crates,' said Jax. 'Imagine how big our hotel will be. Much bigger than Penelope and Winnie's!'

'Jax!' Cora felt suddenly uncomfortable. 'Maybe we should concentrate on making a luxury hotel, rather than a giant one?'

Jax grinned. 'You're right,' he said. 'Anyway, it would take much too long to fill all the crates. How about we take four?'

'Four is a good number,' said Cora. She wiggled her little fingers at him to show she approved.

It took much grunt work and several sprinkles of woodland magic to move four crates over to the brambles and stack them in a cube, two on the bottom and two on top. When they were done, Cora rubbed 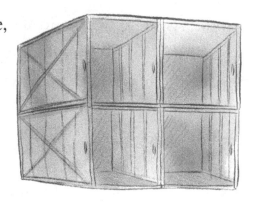 her hands in the earth to rid herself of the feel of the plastic.

'Now for the fun part. Filling the rooms with stuff for the bugs to hide in.'

They looked around, but there wasn't much in the way of natural materials.

'We're not far from Downy Woods,' said Jax. 'We'll have to get the stuff we need from there.'

Cora looked at the sky. The first grey threads of morning light were spreading like cracks in the dark. Was there time to finish their task and get home before sunrise?

# Chapter Four

C ora's heart hammered like a
woodpecker as she and Jax ran to
Downy Woods. They had to cross back
over the road. It wasn't clear. They hid
behind a lamp post. Cora held her breath
as the car's lights swept closer, illuminating
everything around it. Would the Ruffin see
them, or hear her knees knocking over the
roar of the smelly engine? Jax's eyes shone
as the car whooshed past.

'I hope Grandmother Sky's car goes
that fast!'

# Woodland Magic

Scarlet was building Grandmother Sky
an eco-friendly car, powered by a mixture of
forest berry juice and woodland magic.
It was a birthday present. Grandmother
Sky was very old and couldn't walk so far
these days.

Cora pulled a face. 'Jax! What do
you think?'

Jax stuck his tongue out at her. 'Guess
that's a no!'

They reached the woods and began
picking up things to put in their bug hotel.
Pine cones, strips of rotting bark, twigs,
leaves, stones and dried plant stems all went
into their woodland bags.

'That's enough,' said Jax, popping one
last handful of sticks into his bag.

Cora added moss to hers and then
some mushrooms.

'Yum,' said Jax. 'Are they for the party?'

'Leaf and mushroom pizza if we're lucky,' said Cora, fastening her bag.

They arrived back at the supermarket to find Winnie, her back to them, examining their half-finished bug hotel. Cora and Jax crept up behind her.

'Boo!' they shouted together.

Winnie shrieked. 'Sleeping slugs! I thought you were a Ruffin.' Her hands trembled as she showed them to Cora and Jax. 'I didn't touch anything. Keeper's promise. It's huge,' she added enviously. 'Much bigger than ours.'

Jax and Cora exchanged big smiles.

'We won,' said Jax, tapping his thumbs.

Cora didn't tap hers. There was nothing to celebrate yet. The bug hotel wasn't finished and already the sky was turning purple. Sunrise was on the way. She emptied some of her woodland bag out

on to the ground. Jax added the things he'd
collected in the woods and they began to
sort through it all.

'Put the pine cones at the bottom so
we don't have to lift them into the higher
rooms,' said Cora. She rolled a pine cone
over to the crates and pushed it into the
bottom corner. Then she went back for
another one, forcing the two cones together

so that their scales interlocked. The pine
cones were almost as big as her. Cora grew
hot and bothered as she worked. *Would
they finish in time?*

Winnie picked up a dried leaf and stuffed
it in the gap between the cones. 'To give
ladybirds and lacewings somewhere to hide,'
she said.

Cora nodded. She started to add a layer
of moss on top of the pine cones.

In the other ground-floor crate, Jax was
making a twig pile. Cora filled half of it
with stones.

Winnie picked up a strip of bark.
Turning it over in her hands, she said,
'You could use this for a roof, to keep the
rain out.'

'Winnie, that's a brilliant idea!' said Cora.

Winnie looked pleased. 'I could make a
start on it, if you want?'

'Really?' Cora was surprised. 'But what about the competition? If we don't finish our hotel, then you win.'

Winnie shrugged. 'Looking out for the bugs is more important than winning. Our bug hotel isn't very good. Penelope said her head hurt so she couldn't help. I did my best, but . . . When I'd finished, Penelope sent me to spy on you.' Winnie clamped her mouth shut. She looked embarrassed, as if she'd said too much.

Cora eyed her curiously. 'You really want to help?'

Winnie nodded. 'For the bugs, and because you and Jax always make tasks so much fun.'

It was true, Cora realised. She and Jax did have fun together, even though it sometimes got them into a forest of trouble. But they were getting better at not messing things up. 'We'd love you to help,' she said.

Winnie beamed. She gathered up an arm full of bark and, using a little woodland magic, set to work lining the roof. With Winnie's help, they finished the bug hotel very quickly.

Cora stood back to admire their work. The four rooms had different areas with pine cones for ladybirds and lacewings, a stick pile for earwigs, spiders and millipedes, a heap of hollow-stemmed plants for solitary bees to rest in, and stones for the beetles to hide between.

Winnie pushed a strand of yellow hair out of her eyes. She couldn't stop smiling. 'Cattywumps! What fun. But I should go back for Penelope now. We still haven't found any food for the party.'

She turned away, but Cora called her back. Rummaging through her woodland bag, she pulled out the mushrooms. 'Here, take these.'

Winnie looked as if she might hug Cora. 'Thanks,' she said, carefully stowing them away. 'I won't say anything to Penelope about how good your hotel is.' Winnie grinned. 'At least, not until we're back in the Hidden Middle!'

Jax put his woodland bag on his back. 'Time for us to go.'

'In a pip,' said Cora. 'Our hotel just got its first visitor.'

A greyish brown spider with a fat body and long legs was climbing up the pile of twigs. Cora and Jax watched as it squeezed itself into a gap and disappeared from sight.

'Well done, us.' *Now* Cora tapped her thumbs together.

'Good job!' Jax tapped his back.

In the distance, the Horn of Tyr sounded. The ancient Viking horn was a warning to Keepers in the Big Outside that the Bramble

Door was about to be locked. No one
ignored Tyr for fear they would be left in
the Big Outside in daylight, when most
Ruffins went about their business.

'Go!'

'Going!' said Jax.

Cora and Jax ran like foxes, only
slowing as they entered the Whispering
Woods and joined a trail of Keepers

returning home. As Cora hopped over tree roots, she remembered the spider climbing into their twig pile. A warm glow filled her. Their bug hotel was brilliant. They'd found a ton of food for Grandmother Sky's birthday feast. Scarlet would be so pleased. And then she'd make them fully trained Keepers – wouldn't she?

# Chapter Five

'Apple,' said Scarlet, passing it to Haru who was sorting vegetables into boxes. 'Parsnip, swede *and* plum. You have done well!' She smiled at Cora over the wooden counter. They were in the stores — the place where everything collected in the Big Outside was sorted. 'Did you complete your task?' Her look took in Jax, waiting behind Cora for his turn to empty his woodland bag.

'Yes.' Jax nodded vigorously. 'We built the biggest —'

'We finished our bug hotel,' Cora interrupted, before he got them into trouble for turning the task into a competition.

'Hmmm,' said Scarlet. 'A big hotel, you say? I might have to go and see it for myself.'

'Winnie helped with the roof,' Cora confessed. She never took the praise for something that she hadn't done.

Scarlet looked even more thoughtful. 'Hmm,' she said again. 'I hear the Crow's Nest has a fresh batch of daisy cream puffs. Hop along, now.'

'Yum,' said Jax, nudging Cora out of the way to empty out his woodland bag.

Cora's heart slid into her tummy. Not this time, then. They still hadn't done enough for Scarlet to make them fully trained Keepers. Was it because Winnie had helped them? Squawking sparrows! She shouldn't have said anything. *I'm not a cheat!* Cora wouldn't have felt comfortable if she hadn't been truthful. Full of disappointment, she left the stores.

'Still trainees,' she said, when Jax joined her. 'Cattywumps! Are we ever going to impress Scarlet?'

Jax shrugged. 'She doesn't trust us. Our bug hotel was brilliant and I got a *bee's knees* for bringing her fresh beetroot.'

Cora nudged Jax with her shoulder. 'Jax! She only says that when she's really impressed.'

'Want to celebrate with daisy cream puffs?'

Cora thought she'd lost her appetite, but when they reached the Crow's Nest and she saw the puffs, oozing with daisy cream, she changed her mind. They were so delicious, Cora ate three and drank two nettle smoothies. They sat with Trix and Nis, who had saved them a place at their table.

'Hurry up,' Trix urged as Cora licked daisy cream from her fingers. 'The raft race and moonlight party are in two days and I need to check on some things.'

'And we need to practise paddling,' Nis added.

Cora and her friends spent the rest of the day at the river. It was fun, even when Trix kept getting them to haul the raft out of the water so that she could make adjustments.

'Boring,' said Jax, folding a leaf into a water bomb and lobbing it at Cora.

Cora ducked. The bomb hit a tree and exploded. 'Missed!' she giggled. 'Waiting around is boring, but not for Trix. She loves tinkering.'

Nis nodded. 'Every time Trix adjusts something, the raft goes faster.'

'We're going to win,' boasted Jax.

Trix stood back from the raft. Her cheeks glowed. 'We're in with a chance,' she said modestly.

'If we do win, then I vote that Trix keeps the dominoes,' said Cora.

Every year, the members of the team who won the raft race were awarded a wooden medal each and one set of hand-painted stone dominoes.

Trix looked pleased. '*If* we win, then we'll share them,' she insisted. 'Let's get the raft back in the water and try it out again.'

At the end of the day, Trix was satisfied that the raft was ready. They took it out of the water and put it in the Big Barn, where the Keepers gathered for special events.

The following morning, when Cora and Jax arrived at the Bramble Door, they were surprised to find not Scarlet but

Haru giving out the tasks. His sun-wrinkled face crinkled into a smile when he saw them.

'Your task today is to conduct a bug count at your bug hotel,' he said. 'Same for you,' he called out to Penelope and Winnie, queueing a few Keepers behind them.

'Where's Scarlet?' asked Jax.

'Never you mind.' Haru tapped his finger to the tip of his nose. He consulted his leaf notebook. 'Today's Wants are the same as yesterday: food for Grandmother Sky's moonlight party. *Stay out of sight and don't get caught by the Ruffins.*'

He waved Cora and Jax through the Bramble Door.

'It's been raining again,' said Jax as they squelched through the soggy woods.

'I hope it stays dry for the party tomorrow,' said Cora.

'The actual party is always in the Big Barn,' said Jax. 'And it won't matter about the race. We're going to get wet anyway.'

Each year, the raft race ended with all the competitors jumping into the water. It was one of Cora's favourite things to watch and this year she'd be taking part. They came out of the woods and crossed over the stone bridge.

'The river's much higher today.' Cora stopped, hoping to see the otter again or, better still, her cubs. She stood very still, listening for the cubs' squeaks, but all she could hear was the roar of the river.

'Come on,' said Jax.

'Wait!' Cora tilted her head, her pointy ears catching a faint sound. 'I heard something.'

Jax came and stood beside her. The river rushed past, dragging leaves, branches and rubbish with it.

'It's an animal. It sounds scared.' Cora scanned the river. 'There,' she said. 'Oh, Jax. It's an otter pup.'

A short way upstream, in the middle of the river, was a Ruffin chariot. A tiny otter pup sat in the metal basket. It was trying to climb out, but it couldn't. Immediately Cora saw why. The otter's paw was trapped by the mechanism that worked the child seat. The pup's high-pitched squeals jangled Cora's ears as the animal struggled to free itself. If no one helped it, the cub might drown in the fast-flowing water.

'Hold still.' Cora went to jump in the river, but to her surprise, Jax held her back.

'Cora, no! It's far too dangerous. You'll get swept away.'

'I'm a good swimmer.'

'You're a good swimmer in the stream in the Hidden Middle. The river is wider here

and faster flowing, especially after the rain.
Even I wouldn't swim in it,' said Jax.

That stopped Cora. Jax was a daredevil.
'What then?' she asked. 'We can't just
walk away.'

'Hi, Cora, hi, Jax. Is your task a river
one?' Nis and Trix came towards them.
'We've been sent to break up the ground
behind the Ruffin factory to create new

homes for the bugs by encouraging plants to grow there,' Nis added. 'But we thought we'd stop off for some marsh marigolds first. Dad wants them so he can make leaf fries with marsh marigold dip for the party.'

'Nice,' said Cora, her eyes still on the otter. Its cries for help were becoming more frantic.

Jax waved a hand in front of her face to get her attention. 'We could use a branch or something to paddle out to it. It would still be dangerous, but less risky than swimming.'

Cora rounded on him, her eyes wide. 'Something like a raft!'

'A raft would work.' Jax and Cora both looked at Trix.

'What?' said Trix – then she saw the otter cub. 'Oh!'

'It's only a baby.' Cora's words tumbled out. 'It's stuck in the Ruffin chariot.

The water is almost up to the rim of the basket. If we don't rescue it, then it could drown.' She held her breath. It was an oak-tree-sized ask. Trix had been working on their raft for ages.

Trix stood very still. At last, she said, 'Let's go get it.' She set off at a run. Cora, Jax and Nis chased after her. They arrived at the Bramble Door, out of breath, their clothes splattered with mud. Cora had her excuses ready for Haru, but they weren't necessary.

'Granny,' said Trix. 'What are you doing here?'

Trix's granny had long silver hair –

it was plaited and hung over her shoulder.
She stared at Trix over reed-framed glasses.
'I'm standing in for Haru. He's busy getting
things ready for the moonlight party. What
are you doing back so early? Have you
finished your task?'

Trix began to explain, but Cora
interrupted. 'We need some extra tools.'

Granny waved them through the door.
'Be quick,' she said. 'Be back before sunrise.'

# Chapter Six

The raft was in the Big Barn, lined up with all the others. Under Trix's supervision, they lifted it up and squeezed it into her woodland bag. Cora had hoped to carry the raft in her bag, but she didn't let on. It was very generous of Trix to let them use the raft before the race.

Once back in the Big Outside, they lowered the raft into the river. It looked so tiny and bucked wildly in the swollen water. Cora held on to the reed rope, leaning back, using all of her weight to stop the craft from

floating away. Jax had been right, the river
was far too dangerous to swim in. She wasn't
sure about going out in it in a raft either,
but if she was going to help the otter, she
didn't have a choice.

Trix looked equally worried. 'Me first,'
she said, preparing to board.

'Trix, no. It's far too dangerous. I can
rescue the otter pup on my own,' said Cora.

'No, you can't.' Trix, Jax and Nis spoke at
the same time.

'Safer together,' said Trix.

'And faster,' said Nis.

While they were arguing, Jax had
already boarded the raft. He stood with his
legs apart, his long blue hair whirling
around him. He held a paddle in the river,
using both hands, but he was still having
trouble keeping the raft alongside the
bank. 'Who's next?'

'Me!' Nis hopped aboard, closely followed by Trix.

Cora grinned. Her friends were the best. She went after them, but as she jumped with the rope, there was nothing to anchor the raft, so it shot away from the bank. Glancing down, Cora watched the gap between the bank and the raft widen. Would she make it? She landed on the edge of the raft. Trix grabbed her and stopped her from teetering backwards into the water.

'Thanks,' said Cora, her pulse still racing. Quickly, she stowed the reed rope in a neat coil on deck and picked up an

oar. They paddled out to the middle. The
current grew even stronger. The pup's
squeals became higher and more frantic.
Cora paddled harder, her arms burning as
she fought against the river. The tiny otter
was going to hurt itself if it kept struggling.

'Sit still,' Cora called. They were almost
there. She was close enough to see the
otter's whiskery nose and frightened eyes.

'Ready to jump?' Jax asked Cora.

'Ready.' Cora handed her paddle to Jax
for safe keeping. Reaching out, she
grabbed the rim of the trolley with both
hands. The front of the raft lifted out of the
water and crashed back down. Water
sprayed her face. The metal bit into her
fingers, but Cora hung on, blinking the
spray out of her eyes. She'd got this. Cora
took a deep breath as she steeled herself
to leave the raft.

'Hi, lo, GO!' she muttered, then
she jumped.

Her arms were almost pulled out of
her sockets as her body joined them. Cora
paused, taking a deep breath before she
hauled herself up, walking her feet up the
outer side of the basket until she was able
to sit on the top edge. She was almost eye
level with the otter pup. A girl. The pup was
perched on a pile of debris: sludge from the
river, several plastic bottles, a Ruffin bicycle
saddle. Carefully, Cora pushed herself into a
standing position with her arms outstretched
for balance. She walked around the rim of
the trolley, stopping when she was within
touching distance of the pup.

'Hello, you.'

The otter stared back, dark brown eyes in
a fluffy face. Cora edged a little closer. The
pup's whiskers twitched warily. Instinctively,

she pulled away but her paw, trapped under the chariot's hard plastic seat, stopped her.

'Don't struggle. I'm not going to hurt you.' Cora stood very still, giving the pup time to get used to her. Meanwhile, she studied the chariot. The seat opened up when you pulled it, she remembered from Signor Dragonfly's lesson. The Ruffin trolley seat was far too big for Cora to pull open on her own. It would need a sprinkle of woodland magic. Cora pointed her hands at it and imagined it opening. Her fingers tingled and a magical mist fell on the seat. Slowly, it creaked open. Halfway, it stopped. The pup wriggled and the force of the water pushed the seat back again. As it snapped into position, the trolley basket wobbled. Cora threw out her arms to regain her balance.

'Cattywumps!' She tried again, but the same thing happened. The seat moved a pip.

The otter tried to wriggle its paw free,
only for the seat to snap shut.

Cora squatted down. She was scared,
wet and cold and her arms and legs were
aching. She wondered if the otter was
feeling just as miserable. The difference
was, she wasn't trapped and she had Jax,
Trix and Nis cheering her on. A stick
bobbed past. It gave Cora an idea. She
snatched it out of the water. Once again,
she tried to open the seat, sprinkling it
with a magical mist. This time, as the seat
opened, Cora wedged the stick in the
gap, forcing it wider. With a click, the seat
opened fully and the stick dropped onto
the pile of rubbish.

Cora heard a squeak. She caught a
flash of brown fur as the otter pulled her
paw away. The rubbish pile shifted and the
otter pup leapt free. She splashed into the

water, paddling out of the trolley and into the river. Her eyes met Cora's in a silent *thank you* as she swam past. Cora's heart thumped painfully. The tiny pup wasn't out of danger yet. Would she be strong enough to swim across the rushing river to her den?

'Cora, jump.' Jax, Nis and Trix paddled the raft alongside Cora.

Cora hesitated, her eyes on the otter pup, still a long way from the shore. She couldn't leave her yet. A circle of ripples ruffled the water. A sleek head surfaced through them. The otter's mum! Reaching out, the otter mum wrapped her front paws around her pup. The pup squeaked. Mum held her tighter, then swimming on her back, she towed her pup to the bank. A happy glow warmed Cora. She couldn't stop smiling as the otters reached the tree

roots, some dangling in the water, hiding
their bankside den.

'Cora, jump!' yelled Jax again.

The raft came alongside Cora. Jax looked
grim as Nis and Trix and he fought
against the churning river. Cora couldn't
resist one last look at the otters as they
scrambled onto the bank and vanished
under the trailing roots. Now she knew
they were safe, she turned to face the river.
The trolley was higher than the raft. The
raft bobbed wildly, its front lifting out of
the water then crashing back down again.
Cora watched, waiting for the right
moment to jump.

'Hi, lo, GO!'

'Wait!' Jax shouted, but it was too late.
Cora was already plummeting towards
him. A pip later, she realised why Jax had
shouted. A huge branch was coming

down the river. It slammed into the raft and sent it spinning away from her.

'Cattywumps!' This called for a sprinkle of woodland magic. Cora waved her hands, aiming it at the raft to bring it closer, but the magical mist spluttered from her fingers and evaporated. She'd used up too much on the otter pup. She'd have to wait for it to replenish before trying again. Cora splashed into the river. She struck out, swimming towards the raft, but the river was too choppy. She almost swallowed a whole acorn cup of it.

'Urgh!'

'Catch!' Jax held out a paddle.

Cora grabbed it, but the paddle slipped through her fingers. She reached out again, but an empty Ruffin bottle crashed against her, pushing her under. Cora turned a somersault as she sank. Bubbles streamed from her mouth. Hair trailed over her face like water weed. Pushing it out of her eyes, Cora swam up. She broke through the surface and filled her lungs with greedy gulps of air.

Jax, Nis and Trix were yelling something, but it was no good. The river swept the raft further away from her. A twig spun past. Cora caught it. Holding it out in front, like the twig woggles they used in the stream when learning to swim, Cora swam diagonally to the bank. There, she let the

twig go and grabbed hold of a tree root.
Slowly, Cora hauled her soggy self out of
the water. She lay on her back, panting.

Seconds later, Cora heard a new,
terrifying sound. The cheap of a blackbird.
She sat up quickly, squinting upwards.
Purple streaks stained the sky. It was almost
dawn. Cora looked along the river in both
directions. Where were her friends? Her
heart stuttered when she saw a broken
paddle caught in the river weeds. She
fished it out of the water, holding it up to
her face as if the paddle would answer
her questions.

# Chapter Seven

Cora wanted to believe that Jax, Trix and Nis were safe as she clutched hold of the broken paddle. But what if they hadn't made it? What if the raft lay smashed up on the riverbed, and her friends with it? No. She wouldn't think that way. Not until she'd made a thorough search of the area.

Cora took in her surroundings and shivered. She'd come ashore by the Ruffin boathouse and cafe. There were very few places for a Keeper to hide here. The vegetation had been cut back, making way for picnic tables and chairs. Nervously, Cora glanced around, searching for the cafe owner and his bouncy dog. They were often about just before daybreak. The slobbery dog had chased and caught Cora once. She'd been lucky then. Jax, Trix and Nis had come to her rescue.

What was that? Cora swung around, making herself as small as possible as she sheltered behind a dandelion. Footsteps and a mechanical whirring that was growing louder.

Suddenly, the boathouse Ruffin and his dog came round the side of the cafe. With them was a Ruffin child, riding on a bicycle. The bike's headlight flickered. It was attached to a purple basket with a lid. A Ruffin child sat atop, her legs frantically working the pedals. *A Ruffin bike!* If only Jax were here to see it. Cora swallowed. Focus.

The Ruffin stopped to unlock the
boathouse door and the girl cycled on.
As the Ruffin and his dog went inside, he
called out. 'Be careful, Aria. Stay in sight
of the boathouse and don't go near
the water.'

Cora's stomach tightened. The Ruffin
reminded her of her mum, warning her
to stay safe when she was going to the
Big Outside.

'I will,' Aria, the Ruffin child, waved
as she pedalled on.

'Cattywumps!' Cora should have made
a run for it. The flickering headlight made
splotches of light on the grass. Cora froze
like a scared deer. If she moved, the Ruffin
would definitely see her, but if she stayed
still, the Ruffin might run over her.

The bike loomed closer. Aria let out a
cry and braked hard. The bicycle screeched

to a halt less than a flea's leg away from Cora.

*Hopping hares!* The game was up! Cora sprinted for the table. There was a crash as Aria threw her bike to the floor and pounded after her. The bike fell across Cora's path. She leapt back before she was mangled by its spinning wheel.

'Wait.' Aria's hand shot out to grab Cora.

'Not waiting,' panted Cora, dodging around the wheel.

Aria darted after her. 'Please, wait. I won't hurt you.' Her voice, high with excitement, hurt Cora's ears. Terror fluttered like a trapped bird in Cora's chest. The table seemed an oak tree away, but then she noticed a patch of cow parsley. Changing direction, Cora threw herself into it. Green stems topped with cloudy white flowers towered above her as she slid into the middle. There, she leaned against a stem while quietly filling her burning lungs with air.

She had almost recovered when the cow parsley stems swished apart. A huge face appeared. Aria smiled, showing her teeth as she crouched before her. One tooth was missing. Had she lost it crunching on a Keeper? Cora thrust the broken paddle at her. It wasn't much of a defence, but better than nothing. Aria leaned in closer. One of her plaits swung forward, knocking Cora from her feet. Cora landed on her bottom. Aria pounced and scooped Cora into her hands. Still clutching hold of the paddle, Cora scrambled up.

'Are you for real?' Aria's warm breath almost knocked Cora over. 'What's your name?'

Cora stood up tall, her lips firmly pressed together even though she was trembling inside.

'I'm not going to hurt you.'

It wasn't true! Every Keeper knew that Ruffins were the enemy. It was written in *Nursery Rhymes*, a Ruffin book found by one of the Keeper's ancestors. The book was badly damaged, but luckily not the page about Jack Keeper and the Ruffin. *Fi fi fo fum, I smell the blood of Jack Keeper. Yum!* The words played in Cora's head.

Aria stood up. Cora felt sick as the ground moved further away. There was just time to jump. She could use her woodland magic to soften the landing – if it was working again. Cora swung the paddle and whacked it against Aria's fingers.

'Ouch! Ouch! Ouch! Oh no, you don't!'
Aria's hands closed around Cora, locking
her in a finger prison.

There was hardly any room. The girl's
warm skin pressed in on Cora. She jabbed
hard with the paddle. The girl squeaked,
her hands trembled but stayed locked
together. Then she ran. Cora's bones rattled
with each step. Aria's fingers grew hotter and
stickier, but Cora forced herself to press her
face against them. Through a tiny gap, she
watched as Aria slowed as she reached the
fallen bike.

Crouching down, the girl somehow
managed to flip the basket lid open with
her elbow. Then she tipped Cora inside.
Cora ran at the opening, grateful that the
basket was on its side and the lid open.
She was almost free when a stubby finger
pushed her back.

'You're very fierce. I can't hold you, so you can stay there while I get my dad. I can't wait for him to see you. He doesn't believe in fairies.'

'Not a fairy!' growled Cora, lashing out with her paddle, but she was no match for the Ruffin child. The finger held her back and the basket lid snapped shut.

# Chapter Eight

Cora stood in the dark and stamped her feet. How had she been so careless! *Stay out of sight. Don't get caught by the Ruffins.* It wasn't that hard. Not if you were paying attention.

But stamping wasn't going to help. Cora pushed on the lid, growling in frustration when it wouldn't budge. Not even when she put her full weight against it. She wondered how the lid fastened. Was it a buckle, a popper, or did it work by Ruffin magic? No matter. The fastening was far too strong. But maybe if she used some woodland magic to release it?

Feeling hopeful, Cora put her hands up to the lid. She imagined the lid opening. Her magic had refreshed and it crackled and fizzed as it fell in a mist. The lid opened a pip before snapping back into place. Cora tried again, then again. Each time the lid opened a pip before snapping shut. Cora stood back, disappointed. Woodland magic was very useful but not that strong. It could help an injured caddisfly, but it was no use against a stinky Ruffin basket.

The lid rattled. Cora took a step back, watching in horror as it slowly opened. Was it the girl, Aria, back with her dad? Were they going to eat her? Cora gripped her paddle. She wasn't being eaten without a fight. Maybe if she stuck the paddle up

Aria's nose it would make her eyes water
long enough for her to escape.

As the lid widened,
Cora ran forward
holding the
paddle aloft.

'Cora, no!'

Jax, Nis and
Trix scattered
as Cora charged
them.

'You!' Cora
dropped the
paddle. She threw her
arms around her friends, pulling them in for
a group hug. 'You scared
me. I thought the Ruffins were back.'

'We scared you!' Trix snorted. 'First
you nearly drown. Then you get caught
by a Ruffin! We came ashore just after you.

We'd almost caught you up when we
saw the Ruffin grab you. Top marks for
scaring us!'

Cora looked around. 'We should leave.
Before she comes back with her dad.'

A horn sounded in the distance.

'Tyr,' said Trix.

Keepers did not ignore Tyr calling them
home. Cora and her friends broke into a run.
They kept going, crossing the stone bridge
over the river and entering the Whispering
Woods. There, they joined the rest of the
Keepers making their way to the Bramble
Door, until Cora suddenly stopped dead.

'Our task. We didn't even start it and we
haven't found any of the Wants.'

'Nor us,' said Trix.

'You and Nis are fully trained Keepers.
Scarlet will be cross with you, but she
won't send you back to school for not

doing your task.' Cora scanned the forest.
'Wild garlic,' she said, pulling up a handful.
'And mushrooms. Here, Jax, take half.'
Cora gasped as another thought struck her.
'Scarlet's going to be so mad. What if she
doesn't let us compete in the raft race?'

Nis and Jax looked awkward.

'Cora . . .' Trix started to speak, then
stopped.

'What?' asked Cora, her chest tightening
until she could hardly breathe.

Jax continued. 'There
isn't a raft any more.
It crashed into the
branch that knocked
you into the water
and it smashed
to pieces.'

'No raft? Is it
all gone?'

'Most of it,' said Nis. 'What's left is here.' He patted Trix's woodland bag. 'We used the branch like a raft to save ourselves and by combining our woodland magic, we were able to tow the trolley to the bank. The wheels were wonky with rust, but we rolled it to a Ruffin bin and left it there.'

Cora was speechless. The raft was everything to Trix. She'd worked so hard on it. Guilt nibbled her, because she knew that if she had to choose again, she would still help the otter.

'*From nature's floor to our door, caring for the countryside and taking only what we need!*' Trix said, as if guessing her traitorous thoughts. 'Caring for the countryside means caring for the wildlife as well.'

'Trix!' Her friends were the best. Cora hugged her. 'I can't believe that you cleared up the trolley. It was so big.'

'Like Nis said, we combined our magic.'

'But the raft . . .'

'The party and the race aren't until tomorrow evening. There's still time to build a new one. Keepers get the party day off, remember.'

'We'll all help!' said Cora. There wasn't enough time to make the raft as good as the old one, but it was better than not entering the race.

Cora felt as wobbly as frogspawn as she approached the Bramble Door. Would Scarlet be as forgiving as Trix? Unlikely. Once inside the Hidden Middle, they went straight to the stores. Trix and Nis lined up in front of Cora and Jax.

'When Scarlet hears that we didn't complete our task, she might be kinder to you two,' said Nis.

Cora doubted that. Nis and Trix always completed their tasks on time and found tons of exciting things for the stores, but it was nice of Nis and Trix to try to help them. As they waited in the queue, someone poked Cora with a finger. Turning round, she saw it was Penelope.

'You've got river weed in your hair. At least, I think it's weed and not just your straggly hair.' Penelope smoothed back a strand of her own perfectly combed locks. 'And you stink of river mud. We didn't see you at the supermarket. Did you and Jax even start your task?'

'What if we didn't?'

'There's no need to be unfriendly. We only want to help, don't we, Winnie? You can copy our bug count results if you like.' She nudged Cora slyly. 'Then you can pretend that you completed your chore.'

Winnie looked uncomfortable. She flashed Cora a warning look before staring at a spot on the wall.

*Penelope wanted to help? Snoring snails!* Perhaps some of Winnie's good nature was rubbing off on her. Cora was tempted to accept. Then she came to her senses. 'No, thanks. That would be cheating.'

Penelope's expression changed from buttercup-cream sweet to sour-berry bitter. 'Have it your own way. I bet Scarlet sends you back to school. Let's ignore them, Winnie.' She turned her back on Cora.

Now Cora was confused. 'Thanks, but Jax and I aren't cheats.'

'Except the time when we were racing Penelope on the slide and we stuck bluebell jam —' Jax stopped suddenly as Scarlet called Trix and Nis forward.

Scarlet greeted Tris and Nix with an expectant smile that turned to a look of confusion when she saw that, apart from the remains of the raft, their woodland bags were empty. Quickly, Trix explained what had happened, leaving out the part when Cora was caught by a Ruffin.

Scarlet sighed. 'You two always bring me the best Wants so I can't be cross with you, but what about your task? Haru asked you to break up the hard ground behind the Ruffin factory.'

'To help the grass and wildflowers grow back to create new homes for insects and small animals,' Trix added.

Scarlet's face softened. 'Quite right.'

Trix shook her head. 'We didn't have time to start it.'

Scarlet fell silent for a moment. 'You are excused. Saving the otter was far more

important than the task. I'll ask the evening
shift to do it instead. What a shame about
the raft. Would you like to build a new one?
Go and look in the stores.' Scarlet waved for
Trix and Nis to go to the other side of the
counter. 'Take what you need.'

The stores were like a giant natural
museum of sorts, stuffed with things the
Keepers had collected because they could be
useful. If Scarlet had forgiven Trix and Nis
enough to let them look in the stores for
things to rebuild their raft, then maybe she
wouldn't be too hard on her and Jax. Feeling
suddenly hopeful, Cora and Jax took their
turn at the counter.

# Chapter Nine

A long silence followed. It was as if
Scarlet couldn't decide what to do
with the two of them.

'Our task was a bug count,' said Cora
helpfully.

'I went to see your bug hotel,' said
Scarlet, at last.

'You did?' Cora and Jax exchanged
glances.

When Scarlet had said she might go
and see the hotel for herself, Cora hadn't
realised that she was serious. Scarlet rarely

went out in the Big Outside. Then Cora realised something else. Penelope must have seen Scarlet when she and Winnie were doing their bug count. Her offer to share results was made to get them into trouble! No wonder Winnie had looked so awkward.

'I did,' said Scarlet. 'It was impressive. However, this isn't the first task you've failed to complete on time.' She sighed. 'You will go back tomorrow and do your bug count then.'

'Tomorrow, the day of the moonlight party?' Jax asked.

'The very same day.'

Jax looked unimpressed, but Cora said quickly, 'Thank you. We promise not to let you down.' She didn't care that everyone else had the day off. Scarlet had given them another chance and for that, Cora was grateful. 'Come on,' she said, handing over the wild garlic and mushrooms, before hurrying Jax away.

Jax sighed. 'Let's go to the Crow's Nest. I'm hungry for honey-dipped bark-bread toast with a fizzberry smoothie.'

'Later,' said Cora firmly. 'Right now, we're building a raft.'

'Raft building is good too.' Jax cheered up.

For the rest of the day, Cora worked extra hard with Trix, Nis and Jax, trying to make up for her part in the destruction of their original raft. Nis and Trix had found lots of useful bits of wood, twine and bark in the stores and by the evening, the new raft was almost finished.

Cora walked around it critically. 'It's not as good as the other one. It doesn't have a canopy.'

'It's fine,' said Trix briskly. 'It needs a few more tweaks. Nis and I can make them tomorrow when you're out rewilding. We should get to bed now.'

At home, Cora set her solar-powered petal alarm for extra early. As she snuggled under her leaf duvet, Nutmeg, her pet mouse, jumped through the window and sat on the end of her bed. Cora fed Nutmeg

a sunflower seed from the twig pot she
kept them in.

'Scarlet's given me and Jax another
chance to prove we can be fully trained
Keepers,' Cora told Nutmeg as she closed
her eyes. 'We can't mess up again.'

Cora fell asleep immediately.

The following morning, Scarlet met them at
the Bramble Door. It felt weird and a little
scary leaving the Hidden Middle to work in
the Big Outside on their own.

'*Stay out of sight and don't get caught by the
Ruffins*.' Scarlet's eyes bored into Cora's as
she delivered the Warning. *Had she found out
what had happened?*

'We will.' Cora kept a special lookout
for stray Ruffins as they ran to their bug
hotel. When they got there, she could hardly
believe her eyes.

'Jax, look!'

The hotel was teaming with bugs. Ladybirds and lacewings were tucked in the gaps between the fir cones; woodlice and earwigs hunkered down in the stick pile; in each of the hollow plant stems, a single bee snoozed and Cora counted eight beetles in the room packed with stones.

Cora and Jax pulled out their leaf-page notebooks and carefully recorded every single creature staying in the hotel. When the bug count was complete, they tidied their notebooks and pencils back into their bags. Scarlet hadn't asked for any Wants, but the Ruffins had left more wonky fruit and vegetables by the bin.

'Shame to waste it,' said Cora as they squeezed apples, pears, cabbage and squishy tomatoes into their bags.

'Especially when Nis's dad could use it,' agreed Jax, rubbing his tummy.

On the way home, Cora asked if they could stop at the river to check on the otters. Since the rain had stopped, the water level had fallen. The otters were hidden away. Cora and Jax sat on the edge of the bank, listening to the cat-like mewls of the cubs playing in their den.

'We should go,' said Jax at last.

'One more pip.'

Cora hadn't taken her eyes off the tree roots covering the entrance to the otters' home. Suddenly, she squeaked like an otter pup. 'Jax, look!'

A whiskery nose followed by a sleek head peeped out. Cora and Jax stayed very still as

the mother otter sniffed the air for signs
of danger. Finding none, she came out of the
den with her three cubs scampering behind
her. The river rippled as they dived in and
swam a little way out. Cora felt fizzy with
excitement as the cubs played, splashing
one another as they practised swimming
and diving.

'Cora.' Jax tugged her sleeve. 'We have
to go. Trix and Nis need us.'

'The race is tonight!' Cora had almost
forgotten.

'And Grandmother Sky's birthday party.
I can't wait to see her new car.'

'Good haul, today.' Jax patted his
woodland bag.

'Very good haul. And we completed our
task. Jax, do you think . . . ? Cora couldn't
finish as they set off for home. She wanted
to become a fully trained Keeper so badly.

# Chapter Ten

It was Haru waiting at the Bramble Door to let Cora and Jax back in to the Hidden Middle. His face lit up when Cora asked where they should put the food they'd collected.

'Scarlet never mentioned that she'd given you any Wants.'

'She didn't,' said Jax.

'The food was too good to leave,' Cora added.

'Did you finish your task?'

'Yes.' Cora and Jax handed over their notebooks.

Haru glanced at the bug survey. 'Good job! Very good job!' He tapped his thumbs at them. 'And food too. Take it to the Crow's Nest so it can be used for the party.'

Cora's chest swelled with pride, but there was still a nut of disappointment lodged there. Where was Scarlet? Only she could decide if they were good enough to become fully trained Keepers.

The rest of the day passed in a blur of busyness. Cora and Jax worked hard, helping Trix and Nis with the final adjustments to the new raft. Trix was a perfectionist and it was only as the sun fell that she finally declared the raft to be ready. It wasn't a patch on the old one, but it floated and went in a straight line, which was more than could be said for Penelope and Winnie's raft.

Penelope's voice rang out clearly, shouting instructions as they hit the bank for the umpteenth time.

'It's Penelope's fault,' said Trix in a low voice. 'If she paddled harder, the raft would go straighter and they wouldn't keep crashing.'

Cora turned away. While they'd been working, all of the Hidden Middle Keepers had gathered at the stream. Some watched from the bank. Cora and her friends joined the ones entering the race, paddling their raft to an imaginary line across the water, where they waited for the race to start.

Jax tapped Cora's arm. 'Listen!'

Cora could hear it too – a quiet chugging that was growing louder. Two beams of light burst through the trees. Cora's breath caught in her throat as a car came towards her. Sitting tall and proud in

the driving seat was Scarlet. In the back,
flanked by the prince and princess, sat a
smiling Grandmother Sky. The crowd went
wild, cheering and waving. It parted in the
middle, allowing Scarlet to drive right up to
the edge of the stream.

Cora couldn't take her eyes off the car.
She'd seen it once before, when it was
almost finished. The car had been in Scarlet's

workshop when she and Jax had gone there to borrow some things to help them rescue a deer in danger. The finished car seemed bigger and much grander. Made from wood, it had huge wooden wheels, long running boards and a soft leaf roof. The roof had been folded back so that everyone could see the queen.

Grandmother Sky waved regally. She wore a floaty dress made from petals that shimmered in the moonlight. She sat straight, her long grey hair piled on top of her head and studded with her favourite flowers, pink ragged robin. A smile lit up her wrinkled face.

*She looks beautiful*, thought Cora.

Grandmother Sky also seemed very comfortable, resting on the spongy moss-green seats. Cora looked over at Trix proudly. It was Trix who'd found the moss.

'Aren't the headlights great?' Jax could hardly contain his excitement.

'The headlights are perfect.' They were made from the two halves of an empty wood-pigeon egg that she and Jax had found. Scarlet had filled them with starlight-powered glowing flower petals and they lit up the dark with a silvery beam.

The car stopped. Grandmother Sky stood up. It was time for the raft race. A crescent moon, flanked by glittering stars, lit the brook as Cora, Jax, Trix and Nis waited at the start, now a real line of glittering light reflecting on the water from the car's headlights.

Cora spotted her mum watching from the bank with Jax and Trix's parents and Nis's dad. Her chest tightened as she waited for the Horn of Tyr to sound. It was the only time the horn was used, other than to call the Keepers home from the Big Outside.

Grandmother Sky led the crowd in a countdown. 'Hi, lo, GO!' Tyr sounded and the race began.

Cora paddled for her life. She focused on the task, ignoring the splashing, shrieking and cheering around her. Grandmother Sky followed the race in her car and the crowd tagged along behind. Cora's arms ached, but she was determined to do her best for Trix. It was a closely fought race. They almost came third, but they lost ground swerving to avoid Penelope and Winnie, whose raft was weaving from side to side.

As they crossed the finish line, a plaited ribbon of grasses floating on the water, Cora felt terrible. 'Sorry, Trix. Not even a medal.'

'Don't be.' Trix waved her paddle triumphantly. 'It was fun and now we've got the moonlight party. And anyway, the best part of the race is the next bit. Let's jump!'

With a colossal splash, Cora, Jax, Nis and Trix threw themselves into the stream.

'Water fight!' cried a voice.

It was the fiercest and best water fight Cora had ever had. Laughing and squealing, she splashed around, spraying her friends and getting blasted with water back. When everyone was completely soaked, they scrambled from the stream. They left their rafts under a majestic beech tree, home of Grandmother Sky's palace. Flower-petal flags flew from the palace's turrets. Garlands of ivy decorated the staircase

that spiralled around the tree's trunk. The square clearing that the tree stood over was lit with starlight-powered petal lanterns on sticks.

'The decorations are lovely.' Cora pushed her wet hair over her shoulders to see better. Her favourites were the dip-dyed pine cones strung between the trees, and the feather-and-leaf bunting hanging from the Big Barn and the wooden bridge over the brook.

Jax nudged Cora. 'The moonlight party is about to start.'

Grandmother Sky had left her car and was standing in the middle of the bridge. Scarlet stood beside her. She raised her hand and at once the chatter and laughter stopped.

'Happy Birthday, your majesty.' Scarlet's voice rang out in song. Everyone joined in, singing the Keepers' birthday song that

ended with the singers pairing up to cross
hands and do a celebratory spin.

Cora and Jax spun each other round
so fast they landed in a dizzy heap. They
scrambled up as the crowd quietened down
to listen to Grandmother Sky's customary
birthday speech.

'Thank you. I won't keep you long,'
said Grandmother Sky, making everyone
laugh. Grandmother Sky gave thanks to the
countryside, for all that it provided, and to
the Keepers for continually caring for it. She
also thanked Scarlet for the wonderful car –
'My best-ever birthday present.' And finally,
Grandmother Sky read out the names of the
Keepers who had been written in her special
book for finding the best things for the stores.

'These Keepers are invited to my next
palace party,' said Grandmother Sky. She
read out six names, ending with, 'Trix

Wiseowl, for finding the moss for my very comfy car seats.'

Cora tapped her thumbs together extra hard for Trix. She totally deserved her place at the party. The medals for the raft race were presented next and then Scarlet had one last announcement.

'I don't want to spoil the celebrations with this news, but Grandmother Sky agrees that it is necessary as, along with myself, she feels personally responsible for your safety. Yesterday, one of our young Keepers and her friends saved an otter pup from drowning. Unfortunately, she was then captured by a Ruffin.' Scarlet paused as everyone gasped, including Cora. How had Scarlet found out?

'That Keeper was brave and sensible. She kept her wits about her, both when she nearly drowned and again when she was captured. So did her friends, who rescued her

from the Ruffins. Caring for the countryside
*and each other* is at the heart of everything we
do. Those Keepers put themselves in danger
to help an animal friend. For that reason,
I have an extra award to present tonight, a
new prize that will be awarded every year
from now on: the Keeper Teamwork Award.
Congratulations to Trix, Nis, Jax and Cora.
You are our first award winners.'

The Keepers went wild, cheering and
tapping their thumbs together. Cora felt like
she was floating as she, Jax, Trix and Nis were
each presented with a wooden medal strung
on a plaited grass ribbon. It wasn't the medal
she'd hoped they'd win, but this prize felt
even more special.

Scarlet looped the medals around their
neck, saying to each of them, 'Please, stay safe
in the Big Outside, no drowning, stay out of
sight and *don't* get caught by the Ruffins again.'

As the crowd drifted towards the Big Barn for the feast, Scarlet took Cora and Jax to one side. 'I've had my doubts about you two. Mischief is your shadow. I needed to be sure that before I made you fully trained Keepers, I could trust you completely. I'm delighted to say that over the last few weeks you have proved my misgivings wrong. Your bug hotel was the best one I have ever seen. The insects love it. Congratulations. I'm now happy to pass you as fully trained Keepers. Carry on with the good work.'

As Scarlet strode away, Cora and Jax exchanged huge grins.

'Keepers,' said Cora.

'Fully trained,' Jax added.

'Trix and Nis will be thrilled. Let's go tell them.'

'Celebratory spin first!' Jax held out his hands. 'Then after telling Trix and Nis, let's have raspberry fizz and a slice of Grandmother Sky's birthday cake. Nis said it's in the shape of the new car and it's filled with jasmine and honey cream.'

'Yum,' said Cora. 'Race you there.'

'I win!' Jax had already gone!

'Cheater!'

Jax hadn't waited for the spin. Cora didn't mind. Now they were fully trained Keepers, they were both winners.

*The End*

**Building a Bug Hotel**

### Create your own Bug Hotel

Bugs are really good to have around, even the scary looking ones. They play an important part in the food chain by pollinating plants, helping the fruit and vegetables we grow stay healthy and providing food for other bugs and animals to eat. We can all help bugs to thrive by providing them with a safe place to rest and

live. These places are called bug hotels. They can be very simple or grander, like the one Cora and Jax made. Here are two examples of a simple bug hotel that you could make.

**Things You Will Need**

- Small logs/branches
- Rotting wood
- Twigs
- Pine cones
- Dried leaves
- A quiet space, somewhere like a corner of a garden or your school grounds.

## Build a Luxury Log Lodge

★ Find a quiet shady spot outside.

★ Make a pile with the small logs or branches. You could even build it in the shape of a house or pyramid.

★ Add the rotting wood and twigs.

★ Stuff dried leaves in the gaps.

Your luxury lodge is now ready for insects such as centipedes, woodlice and beetles to move in. You may also find that frogs, birds and hedgehogs like it too.

## Build a Perfect Pine-cone Palace

* In a quiet spot, like a corner of a garden or of your school grounds, build a mound or tower of pine cones.

* Gently push the pine cones close together, so the scales interlock.

* Fill any gaps with the dried leaves.

You now have a pine-cone palace fit for ladybirds and lacewings.

## Julie Sykes

As a child, Julie was always telling tales.
Not the 'she ate all the cake, not me' kind,
but wildly exaggerated tales of everyday
events. Julie still loves telling stories and
is now the bestselling author of more
than 100 books for children of all ages
and is published around the world. She
has recently moved to Cornwall with
her family and a white wolf – cunningly
disguised as a dog. When she's not writing
she likes eating cake, reading and walking,
often at the same time.

## Katy Riddell

Katy grew up in Brighton and was obsessed with drawing from a young age, spending many hours writing and illustrating her own stories, which her father (award-winning illustrator Chris Riddell) collected. Katy rediscovered her love for illustrating children's books after graduating with a BA Hons in Illustration and Animation from Manchester Metropolitan University. She loves working with children and lives and works in Brighton.

# Protecting nature is magic for the secret little Keepers

The adventures of the Nature Keepers

**Woodland Magic**

FOX CUB RESCUE

JULIE SYKES
illustrated by KATY RIDDELL

The adventures of the Nature Keepers

**Woodland Magic**

DEER IN DANGER

JULIE SYKES
illustrated by KATY RIDDELL

**Woodland Magic**

THE STRANDED OTTER

JULIE SYKES
illustrated by KATY RIDDELL

Look out for more adventures from the Nature Keepers.

'That's it. Time to go.' Cora emptied the leaves from her net into her woodland bag.

'But we've only cleared the floating leaves,' said Jax. 'There are still loads around the pond's edge.'

'Clearing the pond and the ground around it is a big task. Scarlet said we could have longer if we needed it.' Cora glanced at the sky as she added the net to her bag. The dark was melting away. Soon, the sun would be up and with it the Ruffins, stomping around on their huge pongy feet. She shivered, remembering how only a few weeks ago a Ruffin child had caught and trapped her. Luckily for Cora, her friends had found her and helped her to escape, but it wasn't an experience she wanted to repeat.

Cora fixed Jax with a look. 'If we don't leave now, we might not make it back to the Bramble Door before sunrise. We'll be locked out of the Hidden Middle in daylight!'

Cora and Jax had been working on Downy Common, the furthest they'd ever been from the Whispering Woods. Scarlet had sent them there because she'd finally promoted Cora and Jax from trainees to fully trained Nature Keepers.

Jax gave in. He put his net and rake in his woodland bag then slung it on his back. 'Race you home. Hi, lo, GO!'

They ran across the common and sprinted across a neighbouring corn field. The corn had been harvested and the field ploughed. Cora and Jax jumped from furrow to furrow as they ran towards a derelict barn

on the edge of the neighbouring field. As
they approached, a shape appeared in the
barn doorway.

'Ruffin!' Cora felt as if she was living
a nightmare. She dived, flattening herself
in the middle of a furrow, and hoped that
the earthy ridges would be tall enough to
hide her.

Jax landed a little way ahead of her. He
wriggled back. 'I thought you were tricking,'
he panted, 'cos I was winning.'

'Shhh!' said Cora, wondering if the
Ruffin would hear them. Ruffins had funny
rounded ears that didn't work as well as
Cora's pointed ones, but even so! She forced
herself to breathe slowly and more quietly.
'What's he doing?' she whispered. 'Scarlet
said the barn wasn't used any more.'

Jax raised his head a pip. 'No idea. Unless
he's up early to watch the sun rise. Trix and

Nis saw some Ruffins up on Downy Hill when they were working there a while ago.'

'They should stay in their houses until daylight!' grumbled Cora. Luckily, the Ruffin was going in a different direction to Cora and Jax. Cora stood up. Now some of the danger was over, she noticed something else. 'Corn on the cob with husks! Scarlet will love these.' Cora snatched up the left-behind pieces of corn complete with their long whiskery outer leaves. She handed some to Jax and stowed the rest in her woodland bag.

'Let's have a look in the barn,' said Jax. 'See if we can work out what the Ruffin was doing there.'

'Jax, no!'

Jax ignored Cora and sprinted over to it. The door was open a little and he slid inside. Cora's chest tightened until she could hardly breathe. Ruffins spelled trouble, but Jax was her best friend. She couldn't let him investigate alone. Forcing her legs to work, she followed him inside. The barn was dusty and dark. It smelt of rotten wood, dusty old straw and something else . . .

Cora's stomach turned over. Ruffins! A whole family, camping in the barn.